John MacPhilpin

The Apparitions and Miracles at Knock

The Official Depositions of the Eye-Witnesses

John MacPhilpin

The Apparitions and Miracles at Knock
The Official Depositions of the Eye-Witnesses

ISBN/EAN: 9783337331207

Printed in Europe, USA, Canada, Australia, Japan

Cover: Foto ©Andreas Hilbeck / pixelio.de

More available books at **www.hansebooks.com**

THE

APPARITIONS

AND

MIRACLES

AT

KNOCK.

ALSO,

The Official Depositions of the Eye-Witnesses.

PREPARED AND EDITED

BY

JOHN M̲A̲cPHILPIN,

TUAM.

DUBLIN:

M. H. GILL & SON, 50 UPPER SACKVILLE-ST.

1880.

PREFACE.

———◆———

THE desire to possess a permanent and reliable record of the wonderful events connected with Knock Church, in the county Mayo, has been growing in the minds of all who have paid a visit to the venerated spot, or who have read the accounts regarding it, published in the journals of the day. This desire is not special to Irishmen; it has extended to England, Scotland, to America, and, we can add, to Australia—to every part of the globe in which the English language is spoken.

The Editor wishes to satisfy this laudable desire, and therefore he has prepared this volume. His recompense will be the good wishes of his readers, and of those devout souls who come to Knock, or who hold the name and dignity of Our Blessed Lady in veneration.

The official testimony of those who witnessed the first Apparition is here given, in order to give the reader the best reliable and authentic evidence. Other visions have been witnessed, and lights of a supernatural kind, since the first day of the present year, but of these there is no official testimony yet given.

Tuam, Lady Day, 25th March, 1880.

CONTENTS.

———◆———

CHAPTER

CHAPTER VII.

CHAPTER VIII.

APPARITIONS AT KNOCK.

CHAPTER I.

INTRODUCTORY.

With feelings and views of a character quite opposite in their kind, Catholics and non-Catholics will peruse the following pages. The work will, no doubt, be sought after with equal avidity by persons of every class and of every shade of religious belief. By many, the record of facts will be scanned with a scrutinising eye, and with views and wishes different entirely from those by which the masses of the simple, yet intelligent people are usually influenced. It will, however, be a source of great satisfaction to most people to learn the truth—regard it as they will—concerning the events which have occurred at Knock, a spot now suddenly become famous.

What People think.

Many religious-minded persons doubt the reality of this, let us suppose, supernatural manifestation; the learned dismiss the subject with a smile; some nod the head at the credulity and simplicity of certain people; physicists and men who make science the only criterion of truth, and its evidence the only motive of arriving at certainty in matters supernatural as well as in things natural, will pronounce, in a semi-dogmatic tone, that the apparition has been the effect of some natural cause unknown to man; or that all the witnesses who bear testimony to what they assert they saw, have in some way or other been themselves deceived. On the other hand, thousands of people, at home and abroad, will be convinced—as most persons who have visited the site have been convinced—that the Apparition was, in its appearance, a reality, objectively present to the gaze of the different persons who beheld it; and that it could not, by any possibility, have been produced by human agency.

Opinions do not undo facts.

Whatever the views may be of those who read these pages, they in no way concern the editor of this pamphlet, which is simply a reproduction, in book form, of the facts that he has already published. One need not conceal the fact that the *Tuam News* was the *medium* through which the public learned, for the first time, the story now so well known regard-ing the Apparition seen at Knock on the 21st of August last. The correspondent of the *Daily News*, London, puts this point prominently forward in the issue of that journal, Satur-day, 28th February, just passed. "Publicity," says he, "was first given to the alleged occurrence in the *Tuam News* of the 9th January, and then in a cautious, hesitating manner, accompanied by an intimation that the ecclesiastical autho-rities had up to that time pronounced no final opinion." Every child of Mother Church knows full well that she has been always, and at all times, cautious in giving her sanction to any new apparition or vision, or to any new devotion. She knows, in the words of Gamaliel, the Jewish doctor of the law, "that if this design or work be of men, it will fall to nothing; but if it be of God, you are not able to destroy it:" and time only will more strongly confirm its truth.

The Editor's duty.

As the proprietor of the *Tuam News* was the first to present an account of the Apparition, it is only carrying out his views more fully to be the first also to reissue all that he has hitherto published, and to put the whole record of the varied events in a permanent form into the reader's hands.

It is well always to avoid the expression of any personal opinions, and accordingly the writer will follow the prudent course adopted by the learned correspondent of the *London Daily Telegraph*, who, in his essay—"A Mayo Lourdes"—published March 1st, 1880, says: "It will be my care to express no opinion on the matter in hand, nor even to suggest that I have formed one; the more because from the very nature of the case, what anyone thinks about it is neither proof nor disproof. I shall narrate a plain, unvarnished tale, and for the rest disclaim responsibility."

And, indeed, the mere narration of the facts is quite sufficient. There is already a great religious excitement created in this country and in England, and beyond the Atlantic, too, as is evident from the tone of the journals published in these countries; Irish men and women, from London and from New York, manifest, in their letters, the highest degree of religious warmth on the subject, and appear full of enthusiasm.

The Apparition congruous.

A respected and intelligent correspondent, writing from the south of London, expresses his conviction, apart from the actual proofs now furnished, that the vision has been seen at Knock; "for," says he, "it was only congruous that our Blessed Lady should manifest her presence in some remarkable way to her devout and devoted children in Ireland."

France has been doubly honoured by her presence

Lourdes, a town in the Upper Pyrenees, has been rendered blessed and famous by her appearing at the Grotto de Massabielle, to a poor peasant child, Bernadette Soubirous, daughter of a poor miller of that remote little town. Previously La Salette was favoured in a remarkable manner by her coming. The Poles and the Germans have had supernatural manifestations vouchsafed to them at Marpingen and Dittrichswalde. The religious fervour of Belgium is ever in a glow by the living presence amongst them of one whose daily life is a continuous miracle—Louise Lateau. Why, then, should not faithful Ireland, so devoted to the Saviour of mankind and to his holy Mother, be similarly favoured by her heavenly presence ?

———————

CHAPTER II.

THE Church of Knock, the scene of the Apparition of the Blessed Virgin, of St. Joseph, and, as the witnesses believe, of St. John the Evangelist, is adjacent to a village of the same name, situate in the diocese of Tuam, in the south-east of the county Mayo, and in the baronial district known as Costello. This barony borders on the county Roscommon, along a line of some twenty-five miles, embracing within its extent the rising towns of Ballaghaderin and Ballyhaunis. Knock lies on the western boundary of the barony of Costello, adjoining that of Clanmorris and Gallen. To those who feel an interest in poor-law unions or territorial divisions, it may be interesting to state that the village lies within the Claremorris Union. Knock-druim-Calry, as the spot was once called, is said by Lewis, the writer of the "Topographical Dictionary of Ireland," to be five miles north-east from Clare, as Claremorris had been called some forty-five years ago. Standing on the line of railway that extends from Claremorris to Ballyhaunis, and looking northwards, Knock stands at the vertex of an irregular triangle, the base of which is the longest side, and that drawn from Claremorris to Knock the shortest, namely, five miles, while the third side to the right, from Ballyhaunis to Knock, is six miles and a half.

In Gaelic, the name "Knock" signifies a hill. The village is surrounded by elevated knolls, which are known by the term "knock," or "druim," or "sliabh," in the language of the Irish people. If one stands on the tower of the small church, and views the country around, he will see these elevations arise around him like huge billows in a deep and boisterous sea. Looking, for instance, to the south-west, he beholds Cnoc-ban, or fair hill; and to the north, "druim," i. e., a ridge, an elevated slope; and to the south-east, the wild and bleak mountain-land, called "sliabh na mbreitheamh," or the mountain district of the judges. The village, which rests embosomed amidst these elevations, is very appropriately called "Knock," because, like Hebron, it is in the heart of a hilly country. The view of the region surrounding Knock is not at all inviting; the country district is bare of trees. To strangers coming from England or France, the region is like one through which a desolating army has passed, no sign of trees or of comfortable farmsteads is to be seen; no rich cultivated meadows or fertile agricultural or even well-tilled tracts. The view to the east and west, as one approaches the village from the south, is bleak and uninviting in the extreme, presenting here and there patches of cultivated farms, and for the rest nothing but bog-land, marshes, or badly-tilled upland potato or corn fields.

A second Lourdes.

A wonderful centre of religious excitement, and a great incentive to faith, has suddenly started into form and favour in South Mayo. For the past twelve months the west of Ireland has been the trysting-place of all who have laboured for the improvement of the condition of the small farmers living on Irish soil. The eyes of all in England, and of friends and foes to the cause of the people at home and abroad, have been turned to the west of Ireland. It is there a flame of political and social excitement has been fanned which is spreading at present all over the entire land, embracing, it may be said, the four provinces. The west at the present moment presents an extraordinary attraction of a higher kind to not alone natives in Ireland, but to all Catholics in these kingdoms, as well as to their brethren on the continents of Europe and America. The Catholic world has heard of the name and fame of Lourdes, once a wild spot, but now frequented by all the world, far away in the mountainous region to the south of France. A second Lourdes has arisen at Knock, a small village surrounded by little hills, from which, as expressive of the natural character of the locality, it is known to the natives as the "village of the hills." It is distant about five miles from Claremorris, which is favourably situate on the Great North-Western Railway. All this, it is useful to state, for the sake of those who are now coming in numbers to visit at Knock, the scene of the various apparitions of the Blessed Virgin, and of St. Joseph and the Redeemer, which have been seen by the natives of that unpretending Nazareth. The multitudes who flock to the chapel, or Catholic Church at Knock, from the surrounding districts are quite as numerous as those that formed the monster meetings which for the past nine months have been held in the counties Mayo, Galway, and Sligo. As the people of the neighbouring towns, and of districts and counties more remote, ay, and the Catholics of England and America, take a great interest in the events that have lately transpired, and which at present are spoken of by everybody in this country—Protestant as well as Catholic—relative to the supernatural apparitions seen at the chapel of Knock, it is right to tell the public all the well-authenticated facts regarding the multitudes, the miracles, and the many and repeated manifestations that appear now to be seen each successive week.

The Multitudes who come to visit Knock.

And first as to the multitudes. A vast gathering of people from all the border towns within a circuit of twenty miles assembled those few weeks past at this unpretending little village; some of the pilgrim travellers started before day, guided by the light of the stars alone, and urged onward by the fervour of their own faith. Some were seen wending their way on foot, others on horseback, while whole families of peasants proceeded on their pilgrimage, journeying on the ordinary country vehicle known as a cart; the better class indulged in the luxury of side-cars, or, as they are known in Dublin by the name, "outsiders;" not a few families from the different towns cut a dash by a tandem drive with the highest available vehicle in these parts, known by the unpretending and not agreeably-sounding name of "drag;" a "hansom" would be quite a novel vehicle in that district. The gathering had, certainly, been enormous, exhibiting, at the same time, an agreeable diversity in the mixed character of the crowd assembled.

The diversity and variety of the Multitudes.

The variety of individual character was co-extensive with the greatness of the numbers that composed the gathering. There, one could behold the blind, the lame, the crippled, the deformed, the deaf, the paralytic—all seeking to be cured, like those whom the Redeemer found at the Pool of Bethsaida, in Jerusalem. Accounts without number have come to our ears of cures effected before Christmas last, and, above all, since that period; and on last Thursday week it is stated that two remarkable miracles were performed on two persons who for years had, from the result of accidental causes, been unable to walk. The man found himself so greatly cured, that he left, it is said, his crutches, and bounded home like the lame man cured before the Golden Gate of the temple of Jerusalem by St. Peter and St. John the Evangelist, " walking and bounding along, and all the while giving thanks to God and blessing God's holy name." Thursday and Monday are the days now set apart for visiting this place ; This conclusion has been arrived at because the Blessed Mother of our Lord appeared first on a Thursday, and again on the first day of the New Year—a Thursday ; and on Mondays not a few miracles have been performed on devotees who came to manifest their devotion for Our Blessed Lady.

The Miracles.

The fame of these miracles, and the story of the various apparitions, too, have gone abroad, and have created an immense amount of conjecture and discussion amongst the people relative to the natural and supernatural world.

What the Children of the Faith think.

The children of the faith see nothing wonderful at all in these manifestations. It is to them something that they expected, or, if they did not actually expect their coming at this time and place, they see nothing incongruous in the fact that they have occurred. The spiritual world is to them like a land with which they are familar from that knowledge which their holy faith supplies, pretty much, as they are not put out of sorts with anything they hear or see from America (a far off land) ; because, in this instance, American life and habits are something with which they are familiar, owing to the fact that their relatives in that country commune with their friends in Ireland, and tell them all regarding themselves and American life and manners in that great republic to the west of the Atlantic. In this way our Catholic people are not at all put about by the narration of miracles or of miraculous apparitions at Knock. They are, by faith, aware beforehand that such things happened before, happen now, and will take place as long as the Church of God is on earth. The angels appeared to Abraham, and walked with him, and talked to him, and directed "him in all his ways." They appeared and spoke to, and brought to a foreign country and back, the grandson of Abraham, Isaac, the father of all the Israelites. The same is true of Tobias and Daniel, the prophets ; and of St. Peter, the head of the Apostles, and of numerous saints in the Catholic Church in Africa, in Rome, and in this island during the gólden age of sanctity in Ireland. What happened once, why not happen again ? It is the same God who ruled and governed mankind then as now ; it is the same Church that points out to her children the way to heaven ; the Irish faithful, like those in the time of St. Columkille, or at a later period, are the brothers of the Redeemer, purchased by his sacred Blood. He loves us as He loved them, and sends his angels to take charge of us, as they took charge of them in days past. These points have been spoken of and canvassed in conversation amongst laity and amongst religious for the past six months. It was only when the matter was described in a former issue of the *Tuam News* that the faithful began to attach any degree of credibility to the facts before that time incorrectly narrated. The *Tuam News* gave a summary of the events that had occurred up to that time, stamped with the appearance of the supernatural. The Apparition of the 21st of August last cannot well be understood without having some notion of the position and form of the little Catholic church in the village of Knock.

The Church of Knock.

The building has no pretension to architectural elegance of any kind nor to the internal beauty such as one would wish to witness in God's house. The plan of the building, if plan it can be called, is in the shape of the letter T, the long limb being about sixty feet, and the cross limbs in breadth about fifty feet. The chancel and altar are grouped at the head where the arms project to the right and left. Standing at the altar and looking down the nave, one beholds at the end a loft or entrance that leads to a tower with belfry, both of which are of modern construction and date. The gold-coloured pinnacle of this tower is the first part of the building that comes in view as one, from a southerly direction, approaches the village in which the church stands. To the rear of the chancel and attached to the gable of the altar, a house, less elevated than the walls of the church proper, has been erected; this additional building, which is entered by a door from the chancel, is known as the sacristy—a house in which the sacred ornaments of the church, and the sacred vessels and every requisite for the altar are kept in safety, by the priests or by their attendants. The gable of this sacristy, in a line parallel to the gable of the church, is the second stone erection between the chancel and the outside world, towards, or at the south-eastern gable. It is well, too, to point out the direction to which this plain wall faces: its front looks straight into the approaching meridian sun at 11 o'clock, A.M.; its right wing points to the south-west; its left wing or branch, to the east by north.

Objections answered.

This is the gable hard by which the first miraculous apparition was beheld on the evening and night of the 21st of August ıast. It is thus seen that there are two gables between the altar of the church and the gable fronting the south-east, and that, consequently, if lights appeared in the church, the reflection from them could never beam on the outside at the foot of the wall of the second gable; above all, direct light could never convey, by any law of optics, images when radiating from a centre, and not passing through any other translucent medium, from which the rays of light might, at a certain fixed and measured distance, carry the image of the

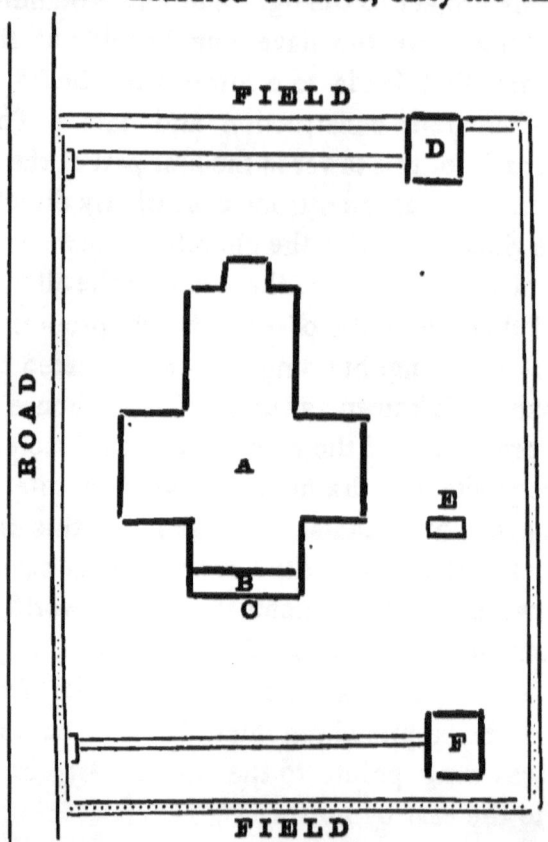

In the foregoing diagram A represents the church; B the sacristy; C the gable against which the (apparition was seen; D the boy's school; E the grave of Mr. O'Grady, the father of the parish priest who built the church; F the girl's school.

object or pellucid picture. The time at which the apparition appeared was some twenty minutes after sunset, so that by no law of radiation from reflected light could the images be thrown naturally or artificially from the clouds. Add to that the great fact, that at the time the Blessed Virgin appeared it was pouring rain in torrents, and the drizzling fall continued the whole time and late onwards through the night. The whole of that day had been one dreary, dismal downpour, from early dawn to the dusky hours of sun-down. We give the following quotation from what we have already written on the subject :—

First account of the Apparition from "Tuam News," January 9th.

" All that may be said in the following lines is an expression of the feelings of the people, and does not pretend to anticipate the judgment which the ecclesiastical superiors may express upon the facts, of which they are already cognisant. The chapel of Knock, at which the apparitions have occurred, is about five miles from Claremorris, and its gilt cross which surmounts the lofty tower can be seen for miles around. The priest who so worthily presides over the parish is the venerable archdeacon of the diocese—the Very Rev. Bartholomew Cavanagh. The chapel is of cruciform shape. The sacristy occupies the upper and smaller shaft, and is immediately behind the high altar. In the gable of the sacristy there is a Gothic window, about five feet by two broad ; its lowest part is about twelve feet from the ground. The remainder of the gable is plain, and covered outside by a good substantial coating of cement to protect the wall from the rains, which beat with great violence, especially upon that side. On this gable wall of the sacristy were seen the extraordinary lights, in the midst of which the Blessed Virgin, accompanied by St. Joseph and St. John the Evangelist, appeared. On Thursday, the 21st of August last, the eve of the octave day of the Assumption of the Blessed

Virgin Mary, was accompanied by a blinding drizzle of rain, which continued till the next day. As some persons were hurriedly going along the road which leads to the chapel, at about 7-30 P.M., they perceived the wall beautifully illuminated by a soft, white, flickering light, through which could be perceived brilliant stars twinkling as on a fine frosty night. The first person who saw it passed on, but others soon came and remained, and these saw, covering a large portion of the gable end of the sacristy, an altar, and to its Gospel side the figures of St. John the Evangelist, the Blessed Virgin, and St. Joseph. On the altar, which stood about eight feet from the ground, and immediately under the window, 'a lamb stood, and rising up behind the lamb was a crucifix with the figure of our Lord upon it. The altar was surrounded by a brilliant golden light, through which up and down angels seemed to be flitting. Near the altar, and immediately to its Gospel side, but nearer to the ground, was St. John, having a mitre on his head, and holding the book of the Gospels open in his left hand as if reading from it. He held his right hand raised, and in the act of blessing, the index and middle fingers being extended after the manner adopted by bishops. To St. John's right stood the Blessed Virgin, having her hands extended and raised towards her shoulders, the palms of her hands turned towards the people, and her eyes raised up towards heaven. To the Blessed Virgin's right was St. Joseph, turned towards her, and in an inclining posture. These figures remained visible from 7·30 to 10 o'clock P.M., witnessed during that time by about twenty persons, who forgot all about the heavy rain that was then falling and drenched them through. The light at the chapel was seen by people who lived near the place. On Monday evening, the eve of the Epiphany, a bright light was again visible, and from 11 P.M. until 2 o'clock A.M. was seen by a very

large number, of whom two were members of the Royal
Irish Constabulary, who were on their patrol duty that evening. One of them said that up to that time he did not believe in it, but he was really startled by the brightness of the
light which he saw. Many cures have been worked through
the intercession of the Blessed Virgin Mary, and by the
application of the cement taken from the chapel wall. We
have heard from the mouths of most trustworthy witnesses
an account of nearly a dozen cures, of which the narrators
themselves were eye-witnesses. In addition to what we have
already written regarding the visions seen at the chapel of
Knock, two remarkable miracles, witnessed by hundreds
of persons, were performed yesterday, namely, sight restored
to two young girls, one of whom had, on the testimony of
her mother, not seen from her birth. She had been several
times with physicians in Dublin, but all to no purpose.
Yesterday, in the presence of hundreds, she received the use
of sight, having visited three times the spot where the Blessed
Virgin Mary is said to have appeared, and after praying
three times in honour of the Mother of God."

Even since these words just quoted have been written,
other miracles, as we have stated in the first part of this
article, have come under the testimony and cognisance of
numbers who have frequented the hallowed spot. His Grace the
Archbishop of Tuam ordered the depositions of the several
witnesses to be taken by a commission of learned priests and
dignitaries deputed for that purpose ; and they have reported
officially that the testimony of all, taken as a whole, is trustworthy and satisfactory.

CHAPTER III.

CLAREMORRIS.

Tourists or travellers coming to Knock must pass through either of the two towns, Claremorris or Ballyhaunis, which are points at the extreme ends of the base of the irregular triangle, of which the village of Knock forms the vertex. The chapel of the Apparition must be reached by car, either from Claremorris or Ballyhaunis—the former is five miles distant, the latter six and a half. In excursion trips the fare, either from Dublin or Athlone, to these towns is the same, and at Claremorris a number of cars are usually at call, ready for all new comers. The accommodation, too, is fair considering the extent of the town, and the means of the inhabitants. The people have been by strangers pronounced civil and obliging. There are in the town two hotels, in which good accommodation can be had, besides private apartments, where families can find themselves at home. All visitors from Waterford, Wexford, Cork, Limerick, and the extreme west and south of Ireland, come to Clare-morris, per the Waterford and Limerick Railway, through Athenry and Tuam, in the county Galway. Cars are to be had at Tuam, from which the journey of fourteen miles can be made in two hours. The fare by public car is two-and-sixpence. What the town of Clare, as it was called in times past, had been forty-five years ago is thus described by Lewis in his " Topographical Dictionary: " "A market and post-town in the parish of Kilcolman, barony of Clanmorris, county Mayo, and province of Connacht, fourteen miles south-east by south from Castlebar, and 117 miles from Dublin." And Kilcolman parish, of which Clare is the capital, he states, contained, in 1837, 8,400 souls, or nearly 1,700 (seventeen hundred) families—at present it contains only 1,300 families. The parish contains 22,886 statute acres. The remains of an old Carmelite convent are found here at Ballinsmala, within one mile and a half of Claremorris. According to Ware, by Harris, vol. ii., 283, the friary was founded in the thirteenth century by the Prendergasts—then owners of the lands in that district. According to an inquisition, held 12th May, 1608, the community possessed twelve acres of land. At the period of the dissolution of monasteries, this establishment and the lands annexed, were granted to Sir John King. The friars were banished; they managed, however, to live as best they could amongst the native Catholics, to whom they were devoted, and who, in turn, held the friars in great veneration. Some thirty-five years ago the friars celebrated Mass within those walls that are now in ruins at Ballinsmala.

Regarding the parish of Kilcolman, or Claremorris, one third of the land is arable, one fourth pasture; the remainder, over one third, is waste or a bog. The boundaries of Catholic and Protestant parishes are the same. The tenants have never been rich. The wealthiest is only so far above want, that one year or two of adverse times, like the present, are sufficient to induce all the privations that come in the train of poverty.

Ballyhaunis.

Ballyhaunis, as well as Claremorris, is favourably situate on the line of the North-Western Railway. It is a rising town. It has two hotels. A growing rivalry exists at present between its inhabitants and those of Claremorris in the marked attention which they pay to visitors going to Knock, and to all tourists and strangers that pass by that way. According to Lewis, it is a market town, situate in the parish of Annagh, diocese of Tuam, barony of Costello. Mayo is divided into nine baronial districts, two of which—Clanmorris and Costello—lie at the south-eastern boundary bordering on Roscommon county. A monastery of Augustinian Friars was founded here in the year 1312, and largely endowed by the family of Nagle, who took the name of Costello, or MacCostello. It flourished till the reign of James I. In the year 1641, the friars gained possession of their old home, and rebuilt portions of the ruined edifice. Again, after a score of years, they were obliged to fly. They continued to dwell amongst the people, for priests in Ireland at that period were obliged to hide from the view of any Government official, and to abide for three months or twelve months in one house, and then to seek a change of habitation, lest their presence in a town or village should become publicly known. The friars administered to the spiritual wants of the faithful, celebrating Mass, whenever possible, in the ruined cloisters of their monastery. Some fifty-five years ago they began again to rebuild the broken walls of their church and convent. They possessed by right over one hundred and fifty acres of land, bestowed by the Barons MacCostellos, in times past, on the community. This property the grandfather of the present Viscount Dillon took to himself at the end of the century just passed, and with much seeming kindness gave the friars, with a lease for ever, at a shilling an acre, twelve acres of their own land, keeping in his own right as lord of the territory around the rest of the fee-farm, which really belonged to the good religious, but to which the English law gave them no title, or rather to which it disentitled them. At the present time the prior and his brethren in religion are in possession of a neat church and of a very substantial establishment suited to a small community. As the Augustinians form one of the mendicant orders, the friars derive their support from the alms and offerings of the faithful, together with the proceeds of the small farm.

What is that?

This passing notice of the monastery has been given to please the legitimate curiosity of the many visitors who make Ballyhaunis their way in going to visit Knock. The first thing that strikes a stranger's eye on entering the town from the railway station is the venerable pile of massive, but ancient-looking, buildings erected on the hill. He naturally asks: What is that? The site is certainly attractive, and the most commanding in Ballyhaunis. It could be rendered still more striking. The town and convent are entwined in historic, social, and religious relations. With the foundation of the monastery for the hermits of St. Augustine, in the fourteenth century, Ballyhaunis grew into existence as a town. Its religious life was supported in days of persecution by the friars, and the names of Jordan, Waldron, Bourke, Fitzgerald, Egan, O'Neil, Dowling, Finn, and O'Hara, to be met with amongst the best-to-do of the inhabitants, show that the priors and friars, who bore those names, were, like most of the Irish priesthood, the sons of the people.

Knock—The Parish Priest—His Dwelling.

A visitor taking car at this town, or at Claremorris, will reach Knock after an hour's drive. The parish is at the head of a union of two, for Aughamór and Knock are united, and both are at present under the pastoral charge of the Very Rev. Bartholomew A. Cavanagh, archdeacon of the diocese. In each of the parishes there is a church. The archdeacon confines his ministrations and personal care chiefly to the parish of Knock, looking after the wants, spiritual and temporal, of the people, and relieving them in their hours of trial, and attending to all sick-calls. In this way the good pastor's time is fully occupied, especially in this year of general want, when the time and patience and power of endurance of every Irish priest in the West of Ireland is fully put to the tightest test. Archdeacon Cavanagh receives some ninety letters each day. It is evident that he cannot attend to the demands of all his present correspondents, and if some of them are disappointed it is not owing to indifference or negligence on the part of the pious pastor. The residence of the venerable archdeacon is quite near the chapel, say about two minutes' walk. It is a plain, thatched cottage, consisting of three rooms and a kitchen. It is in shape and size like the dwelling of some of his humbler parishioners, and is distinguished from the common class of cottages by a flower garden in front of the leading entrance. He receives all those who come to him with great courtesy and kindness, having a friendly word for everyone. Strangers of note, and clerical visitors, are usually treated by him with much attention and marked respect.

Pious Peasants.

Qualis pater, talis filius—like father, like son, is an old adage, and may be turned a little into the following: *qualis pastor, talis grex*—like pastor, like flock The pastor o Knock and Aughamór is zealous, devoted to his sacred calling, an humble client of Mary, the Mother of God; and so the people, at least many of them, are simple in their habits of life, and imbued with a deep-seated love of their holy religion. Like the priest who teaches them, they have great faith in our blessed Lord, and the fullest hope in his saving merits; they are imbued with a deep, devotional attachment to the blessed Mother of the Redeemer. All the peasant Catholics of the West of Ireland regard our Blessed Lady pretty much as they do a respected and honoured member of the household to which each respectively belongs. Christ is their Brother, the Eternal Son of our common Heavenly Father; but Holy Mary, his Mother, is their Mother, and for her their love and veneration is childlike and elevated—childlike in its trust and natural simplicity, elevated in the knowledge they possess of her transcendent perfections, her sanctity, grace, and the marvellous share that was hers in the divine economy of Redemption; and consequently her mighty influence and all-saving power with her Divine Son.

CHAPTER IV.

THE village of Knock is now spoken of not only in Ireland, in England, in Scotland, but in America. Letters from the most distant districts in the far-off United States of the American Continent have been received, in which detailed questions have been put respecting the "apparitions and the miracles" at Knock. It is quite impossible to answer all the inquiries made on the several points proposed, regarding the general subject and the detailed events that have been narrated, and which, it is stated, have actually taken place. The events can well be grouped under two headings, namely, those respecting the Apparition seen on August 21st, 1879, the eve of the octave of the Feast of the Assumption of the Blessed Virgin Mary, and those that tell of the "miracles" that have been wrought since Christmas last. It is easy enough to deal with the question of the first Apparition, because the proofs regarding it rest on the evidence of the witnesses who assert, and even swear, that they beheld it. These are at least fifteen in number.

Reasoning on this point.

How it could happen that fifteen persons of different ages, and of different ways of thinking and of living—persons differing in age, in condition, in place, and position, could, without any apparent reason, conspire to say they all saw a certain thing which, in the opinions of those who do not credit their narration, they did. *not* see, and that they were under that delusion (not one, but all of them) that they saw it, some for one hour, some for an hour and a half, some for two hours, is a thing quite impossible to comprehend. A person can understand how one could be deceived even with his or her eyes open, and the senses quite alive to all things else around and about; but how fifteen could be deceived or could conspire, differing, as they did, in age, state, and condition, is something as marvellous in the moral world as the Apparition itself is in the order of material events. One of three conclusions must be come to by any sensible and rational being who weighs the evidence: Either the Apparition was a reality; or, it never took place; and all the fifteen witnesses have conspired without cause, and have been deceivers; or they all of one accord innocently imagined they beheld what they never saw. Which of the three is the easier to credit: (1) that they saw it; or (2) imagined they saw it; or (3) concocted the whole thing, and were deceivers? The non-Catholic affirms, "there was no such thing as an apparition;" "it is all a hoax." So, too, says the incredulous Catholic; and, mind you, very few learned Catholics yet give any credit to the events that have been narrated. This is fair. It is natural that the people should doubt. It is even right that they should doubt, for every story that one hears ought not to be readily credited. And it always happens that those who doubt longest, like St. Thomas the Apostle, are those who are, in matters of truth, the firmest supporters afterwards of that which they are certain is true. Well, then, in respect to the non-Catholic section of the community and of the Catholics who do not give credit to the story or narration of the first Apparition, one could say: You must (*a*) either believe that the apparition did *de facto* take place, account for its appearance as you will; or (*b*), that fifteen quiet, rational people, while in their senses, and while awake, were deceived; or that, worse still (*c*), they were rogues and cheats prepared quite well enough to combine. The reply given is: "I do not believe they saw the Apparition." Very well. They were all deceived, then, without any fault on their part, or they conspired without cause. If deceived, there have been fifteen miracles instead of one wrought, for it is a wonderful and, indeed, a miraculous thing to make a person seriously believe he saw what he did not see, and to hold him to it for one hour, or two, or longer. No rational being could by human possibility be so deceived, and, above all, convinced *rationally* that the events occurred which, in point of fact (if he were deceived), never had occurred. And then you must multiply that deception by fifteen, for that number of rational, sensible men and women declare that they beheld the apparition, not for a moment, not in a loose, transient way, but in a settled manner for hours, so that they had time to come and go, to think and examine, to see the hands, eyes, and the minutest outline of the beings who stood before them. They endured cold, and rain, and wet, while looking at the vision they declare they saw, but which the man who does not credit the story says they did not see. His alternative is a far greater miracle in itself than that of the believer, for, in his case, it is simply one apparition, in the other, it was fifteen apparitions deceiving each of the rational beings who stood on looking at what had, according to their theory, no reality. If they conspired without cause, there was an additional miracle; for, in matters of lying and deception, it is seldom or ever all can be at one in narrating the same events. Witness the two judges or elders whom the Prophet Daniel examined. Each told a different story when examined separately and apart, simply because each of the two was telling an untruth. Now, in the case of these fifteen witnesses, it is amazing that all of them and each of them tell in substance the same event. How, supposing they were deceivers, and that they conspired, did each hit exactly on the same story when singly examined regarding the vision, the time, place, and circumstances ? They differ, it is true, in minor and special outlines, as all men will, in giving an account of the same event ; but they tell in substance and in integrity of detail the same story. No other conclusion can, therefore, be arrived at regarding the first Apparition than that it actually has occurred. Let men of learning account for it as they like.

Other Conjectures groundless.

The non-believing individuals describe the appearance, either as (1) a miracle; or (2) the effect of reflected light; or 3) some kind of magic-lantern proceeding ; or (4) the effect of phosphorus ; or of (5) electric or magnetic currents ; or (6) natural miasmatic gustations from the earth below, arising perhaps, from a stratification of coal or of petroleum some thirty or fifty feet under the surface. The vision, or the luminous appearances, could not come from reflected lights ; for, as a rule, and as a matter of science, mirages are seen in the clouds, and not at the gables of a house, and they never continue longer than a few moments, like a rainbow, just only while the sun is shining on a certain point. Now, in the first vision at Knock, the Apparitions continued for hours, and was seen both before the sun had fully gone down, and after it had set, in day time and in night time, and that for a lengthened period. What regarding the effects of a magic lantern ? Anyone who has seen the place can behold at a glance that to produce images on the wall at Knock Chapel by magic lanterns is simply impossible. The nearest point at which a performer could stand is distant thirty yards from the gable, and no lens and no electric light known to scientists at the present day can cast fully defined likenesses the size of

a man on four hundred square feet of surface for some
hours in the light of day, and the darkness of night, and that
with pencils of rays of light invisible from artificial
sources of illumination. Neither is the phosphorus
theory of any avail. One would require an immense amount
of phosphorus to daub the whole gable of a church with it.
The phosphorus would ignite in the daytime in the hands
of any unskilled, nay, the most cautious artist. Then, again,
the light of phosphorus could not be seen distinctly thirty
yards off; especially it could not be seen at daytime.
Again, it could not present, with its ever-fitful flame, accurately and minutely defined features. Some of the witnesses
testify that they beheld the very eye-balls of the figures, which,
as Patrick Hill testifies, appeared to him to be those of living beings; he saw, he says, not only the eyes, but the iris
and the pupil. Although some of the witnesses have described the figures as statues, yet they assert that those they
saw were like living beings, as their eyes, and the brightness
of their eyes, ever showed. They were statue-like only in
this respect, that the figures did not speak. It is in that
respect the witnesses bear testimony to their statue or ghost-
like appearance. Phosphoric light is ever fitful and fluctuat-
ing, like the light of a reflected moon on the disturbed surface of a rippling lake. It is never even, nor at rest. But in
the Apparition there was no rippling, or ever and constant
changing of light. The figures and likenesses that were
seen were settled; they presented an accurate outline, and
were constant and continuous in their pose for two hours
and a half. Add to all this that the lights were beheld at a
distance of over half a mile; phosphoric lights cannot be
seen thirty yards off—above all, they cannot be seen in day-
light. But this is certain, that while water is being poured
on a surface on which phosphorus is being rubbed, no light

from it is seen. Now, according to the testimony of the witnesses, it was, during the whole period, pouring torrents of rain on the gable end of the church, so much so, that all of them say what they wondered at most, like Moses looking at the bush burning and yet not consumed, was, that the "bodies" before them were deluged with rain, and all the while they were not wet, nor the silvery glow that surrounded them in any way lessened. The glowing light of phosphor is yellowish; this seen on the night of the apparition was white.

The objection that the appearances have been produced by electric lights is too fanciful. Electric lights do not be made manifest in one part of the earth, without being seen or made manifest under the same circumstances in other parts. If electric lights arise and are diffused around one gable of a church at a certain time and in certain circumstances, what prevents the electric lights from being seen under similar and the like circumstances in other places? Hence it is in itself a kind of miracle to make the electric current, everywhere existing in the earth, tell without special cause in one place and not in another, in like situation. Lastly, about the stratifications under the earth. That is merely fanciful or hypothetic. But suppose there are bituminous substances lying under the church, fifty or sixty feet down under the surface, why do exhalations arise at the gable rather than in any other part? Why do the lights, seen almost each night, increase in bulk as they ascend around the gable and the wall each side? How, too, could well-defined figures be fashioned from any such exhalations?—why does not curling smoke make images continuously for hours?

All that has been said or written has no positive sanction from the Church or from the Church rulers and ecclesiastical guides; that which has been just stated has only the same amount of authority that is usually given to any public event witnessed by many—but with this exception, that much greater care has been taken to be accurate and rigidly truthful in the account[s] now given than if they were the ordinary events of the day. If they are supernatural, as they appear to be, there is much more to be said regarding them ; if, after all, they are in any way unreal, as some think, then very soon that want of reality must come to light. Meantime, till the Church speaks authoritatively on the subject, one has fair grounds for believing the whole account of the Apparition to be true, and th t some, at least, of the miracles are a reality.

———————————

CHAPTER V.

Depositions taken in the presence of the Very Rev. Arch-
deacon Bartholomew A. Cavanagh, P.P.; of Rev. James Canon
Waldron, P.P., Ballyhaunis; and Rev. U. J. Canon Bourke,
P.P. of Kilcolman, Claremorris, Co. Mayo, deputed by his
Grace, the Archbishop of Tuam, to see into the truth of the
vision alleged to have appeared at the Catholic Church of
Knock on the evening of the 21st of August, the octave of
the Assumption of the B.V.M., 1879.

In presenting the testimony of the different witnesses who
beheld the apparitions on the evening of the 21st August last,
the first place is rightly due to the evidence of Patrick Hill,
of Claremorris, a young, frank, intelligent boy, of about
thirteen years of age. His account of the Apparition is the
fullest and most satisfactory. It extends to even the minutest
details. To all who question him, he replies with an open,
childlike simplicity of manner, and with the readiness of one
who knows and who feels that he is certain of what he tells.
He states some points to which other eye-witnesses do not
even allude; for instance, that on the forehead of the figure
representing the Blessed Virgin, he saw just under the circlet
of the crown, and where, on the human head, the hair grows,
a full-blown rose. The other witnesses do not even allude
to this remarkable fact. The palms of the hands were
not turned outwards, but slightly diverging from a parallel position, one palm fronting the other, with a gentle
convergency towards the face of the figure. He observed

the feet, and remarked that the right foot was in advance of the left, like one going to move forward; and that, in fact, the figures did move forward at times, and backwards towards the gable whenever the people drew nearer to them. He saw angels, having their faces veiled, fluttering around the Lamb. Other witnesses say they saw only glittering lights around the Lamb, but that they were not angels. Master Hill declares that they appeared to him to move, and, as it were, on wing, but that he could not see their faces. The cross, he says, was behind the Lamb, and erect on the altar, and not on the Lamb, as is represented. The other witnesses used the words behind the Lamb, on the Lamb; he states with a certain conviction the cross was behind the Lamb, but inward, erect, or perpendicular to the altar, and in no way touching the Lamb. Again, he states that although a luminous whiteness covered the whole gable, or the greater portion of it, yet a dark border line out a little from each of the forms, gave the beholders a clear and distinct view of each of the figures that stood before them: for instance, between St. John and the figure of the Blessed Virgin, a dark or less bright border line showed how far the bright rays that encircled the Virgin extended, and how far those radiating from St. John extended, and the meeting of the two was less bright than the lustrous whiteness that was seen around.

Then, again, he saw, he states, not only the eyes of the Immaculate Lady, but the iris and the pupil in each. That after being a while looking on and gazing at the figures, he went up towards St. John, and could distinctly see the lettering in the book which St. John appeared to be reading.

These are points that are worth noting in the evidence of Master Patrick Hill, on account of their special character, and the minuteness of outline, and the simple certainty with which he tells one out straight what he saw.

No phosphoric or electric action could bring out the distinct brightness in the pupil of the eye, or the minute distinctness in the lettering of the Book of Gospels.

His Testimony.

I am Patrick Hill; I live in Claremorris; my aunt lives at Knock; I remember the 21st of August last; on that day I was drawing home turf, or peat, from the bog, on an ass. While at my aunt's, at about 8 o'clock in the evening, Dominick Beirne came into the house; he cried out: Come up to the chapel and see the miraculous lights, and the beautiful visions that are to be seen there. I followed him; another man, by name Dominick Beirne, and John Durkan, and a small boy named John Curry, came with me; we were all together; we ran over towards the chapel. When we, running southwest, came so far from the village that on our turning the gable came in view, we immediately beheld the lights, a clear, white light, covering most of the gable, from the ground up to the window and higher. It was a kind of changing bright light, going sometimes up high and again not so high. We saw the figures—the Blessed Virgin, St. Joseph, and St. John, and an altar, with the Lamb on the altar, and a cross behind the Lamb. At this time we reached as far as the wall fronting the gable; there were other people there before me; some of them were praying, some not; all were looking at the vision; they were leaning over the wall or ditch, with their arms resting on the top. I saw the figures and brightness; the boy, John Curry, from behind the wall, could not see them; but I did; and he asked me to lift him up till he could see the grand babies, as he called the figures; it was raining; some—amongst them Mary M'Loughlin—who beheld what I now saw, had gone away; others were coming. After we prayed awhile I thought it right to go across the wall and into the chapel yard. I brought little Curry with me ; I went then up closer ; I saw everything distinctly. The figures were full and round, as if they had a body and life ; they said nothing, but as we approached they seemed to go back a little towards the gable. I distinctly beheld the Blessed Virgin Mary, life size, standing about two feet or so above the ground, clothed in white robes, which were fastened at the neck ; her hands were raised to the height of the shoulders, as if in prayer, with the palms facing one another, but slanting inwards towards the face ; the palms were not turned towards the people, but facing each other as I have described ; she appeared to be praying ; her eyes were turned, as I saw, towards heaven ; she wore a brilliant crown on her head, and over the forehead, where the crown fitted the brow, a beautiful rose ; the crown appeared brilliant, and of a golden brightness, of a deeper hue, inclined to a mellow yellow, than the striking whiteness of the robes she wore ; the upper parts of the crown appeared to be a series of sparkles, or glittering crosses. I saw her eyes, the balls, the pupils, and the iris of each— [the boy did not know those special names of those parts of the eye, but he pointed to them, and described them in his own way]—I noticed her hands especially, and face ; her appearance ; the robes came only as far as the ankles ; I saw the feet and the ankles ; one foot, the right, was slightly in advance of the other ; at times she appeared, and all the figures appeared to move out and again to go backwards ; I saw them move ; she did not speak ; I went up very near ; one old woman went up and embraced the Virgin's feet, and she found nothing in her arms or hands ; they receded, she said, from her ; I saw St. Joseph to the Blessed Virgin's right hand ; his head was bent, from the shoulders, forward ; he appeared to be paying his respects ; I noticed his whiskers ; they appeared slightly gray ; there was a line or dark mearing between the figure of the Blessed Virgin and that of St. Joseph, so that one could know St. Joseph, and the place where his figure appeared distinctly from that of the Blessed Virgin and the spot where she stood. I saw the feet of St. Joseph, too; his hands were joined like a person at prayer. The third figure that stood before me was that of St. John the Evangelist; he stood erect to the Gospel side of the altar, and at an angle with the figure of the Blessed Virgin, so that his back was not turned to the altar, nor to the Mother of God; his right arm was at an angle with a line drawn across from St. Joseph to where our Blessed Lady appeared to be standing; St. John was dressed like a bishop preaching; he wore a small mitre on his head; he held a Mass Book, or a Book of the Gospels, in the left hand; the right hand was raised to the elevation of the head; while he kept the index finger and the middle finger of the right hand raised, the other three fingers of the same hand were shut; he appeared as if he were preaching, but I heard no voice; I came so near, that I looked into the book; I saw the lines and the letters. St. John wore no sandles; his left hand was turned towards the altar that was behind him; the altar was a plain one, like any ordinary altar, without any ornaments. On the altar stood a Lamb—the size of a lamb eight weeks old; the face of the Lamb was fronting the west, and looking in the direction of the Blessed Virgin and St. Joseph; behind the Lamb a large cross was placed erect or perpendicular on the altar; around the Lamb I saw angels hovering during the whole time, for the space of one hour and a half or longer; I saw their wings fluttering, but I did not perceive their heads or faces, which were not turned to me. For the space of one hour and a half we were under the pouring rain; at this time I was very wet; I noticed that the rain

4

did not wet the figures which appeared before me, although I was wet myself; I went away then.

(Signed)   PATRICK HILL.

Witness present—U. J. Canon Bourke.
October 8th, 1879.

Second Witness.

I, Mary M'Loughlin, live in Knock; I am housekeeper to the Rev. Archdeacon Cavanagh; I remember the evening of the 21st of August; at the hour of seven or so, or a little later, while it was yet bright day, I passed from the Rev. the Archdeacon's house on by the chapel, towards the house of a Mrs. Beirne, widow. On passing by the chapel, and at a little distance from it, I saw a wonderful number of strange figures or appearances at the gable, one like the B. V. Mary, and one like St. Joseph, another a bishop; I saw an altar; I was wondering to see there such an extraordinary group; yet I passed on and said nothing, thinking that possibly the Archdeacon had been supplied with these beautiful figures from Dublin or somewhere else, and that he said nothing about them, but had left them in the open air; I saw a white light about them; I thought the whole thing strange; after looking at them I passed on to the house of Mrs. Beirne's in the village; after reaching Widow Beirne's house I stayed there half an hour at least; I returned then homewards to the Archdeacon's house, accompanied by Miss Mary Beirne, and as we approached the chapel, she cried out, "Look at the beautiful figures." We gazed on them for a little, and then I told her to go for her mother, Widow Beirne, and her brother, and her sister, and her niece, who were still in the house which she and I had left. I remained looking at the sight before me until the mother, sister, and brother of Miss Mary

Beirne came ; at the time I was outside the ditch and to
the south-west of the schoolhouse near the road, about thirty
yards or so from the church ; I leaned across the wall in order
to see, as well as I could, the whole scene. I remained now
for the space of at least a quarter of an hour, perhaps longer;
I told Miss Beirne then to go for her uncle, Bryan Beirne,
and her aunt, Mrs. Bryan Beirne, or any of the neighbours
whom she should see, in order that they might witness the
sight that they were then enjoying. It was now about a
quarter past eight o'clock, and beginning to be quite dark.
The sun had set ; it was raining at the time. I beheld,
on this occasion, not only the three figures, but an altar
further on to the left of the figure of the B.V.M., and to
the left of the bishop and above the altar a Lamb about the
size of that which is five weeks old. Behind the Lamb appeared the cross; it was away a bit from the Lamb, while
the latter stood in front from it, and not resting on the wood
of the cross. Around the Lamb a number of gold-like stars
appeared in the form of a halo. This altar was placed right
under the window of the gable and more to the east of the
figures, all, of course, outside the church at Knock. I parted
from the company or gathering at eight and a half o'clock.
I went to the priest's house and told what I had beheld, and
spoke of the beautiful things that were to be seen at the gable
of the chapel ; I asked him, or said, rather, it would be worth
his while to go to witness them. He appeared to make
nothing of what I said, and consequently he did not go.
Although it was pouring rain the wall had a bright, dry appearance, while the rest of the building appeared to be dark.
I did not return to behold the visions again after that, re-
maining at my house. I saw the sight for fully an hour.
Very Rev. B. Cavanagh heard the next day all about the
Apparition from the others who had beheld it ; and then it

came to his recollection that I had told him the previous evening about it, and asked him to see it.

NOTE.—Mary M'Loughlin had gone away before Patrick Hill came. Their testimony relates to two distinct and separate times while the Apparition was present. She saw it, like one who did not care to see it, and in a transverse direction, not straight; he saw it directly and fully, and like a confiding child, went up calmly to where the Blessed Virgin stood.

Third Witness.

Testimony of Mary Beirne, aged about 26 years.

I live in the village of Knock, to the east side of the chapel; Mary M'Loughlin came on the evening of the 21st of August to my house at about half-past seven o'clock; she remained some little time; I came back with her as she was returning homewards; it was either eight o'clock or a quarter to eight at the time. It was still bright; I had never heard from Miss M'Loughlin about the vision which she had seen just before that. The first I learned of it was on coming at the time just named from my mother's house in company with Miss Mary M'Loughlin, and at the distance of three hundred yards or so from the church, I beheld, all at once, standing out from the gable, and rather to the west of it, three figures which, on more attentive inspection, appeared to be that of the Blessed Virgin, of St. Joseph, and St. John. That of the Blessed Virgin was life-size, the others apparently either not so big or not so high as her figure; they stood a little distance out from the gable wall, and, as well as I could judge, a foot and a half or two feet from the ground. The Virgin stood erect, with eyes raised to heaven, her hands elevated to the shoulders or a little higher, the palms inclined slightly towards the shoulders or bosom; she wore a large cloak of a white colour, hanging in full folds and somewhat loosely around her shoulders, and fastened to the neck; she wore a crown on the head—rather a large crown—and it appeared to me somewhat yellower than the dress or robes worn by Our Blessed Lady. In the figure of St. Joseph the head was slightly bent, and inclined towards the Blessed Virgin, as if paying her respect; it represented the saint as somewhat aged, with gray whiskers and grayish hair. The third figure appeared to be that of St. John the Evangelist; I do not know, only I thought so, except the fact that at one time I saw a statue at the chapel of Lekanvey, near Westport, county Mayo, very much resembling the figure which stood now before me in group with St. Joseph and Our Blessed Lady, which I beheld on this occasion. He held the Book of Gospels, or the Mass Book, open in his left hand, while he stood slightly turned on the left side towards the altar that was over a little from him. I must remark that the statue which I had formerly seen at Lekanvey chapel had no mitre on its head, while the figure which I now beheld had one—not a high mitre, but a short-set kind of one. The statue at Lekanvey had a book in the left hand, and the fingers of the right hand raised. The figure before me on this present occasion of which I am speaking had a book in the left hand, as I have stated, and the index finger and the middle finger of the right hand raised, as if he were speaking, and impressing some point forcibly on an audience. It was this coincidence of figure and *pose* that made me surmise, for it is only an opinion, that the third figure was that of St. John, the beloved disciple of our Lord. But I am not in any way sure what saint or character the figure represented. I said, as I now expressed, that it was St. John the Evangelist, and then all the others present said the same—said what I stated. The altar was under the window, which is the gable, and a little to the west near the centre, or a little beyond it. Towards this altar St.

John—as I shall call the figure—was looking, while he stood at the Gospel side of the said altar, with his right arm inclined at an angle outwardly, towards the Blessed Virgin. The altar appeared to me to be like the altars in use in the Catholic Church—large and full-sized. It had no linens, no candles, nor any special ornamentations; it was only a plain altar. Above the altar, and resting on it, was a Lamb, standing with the face towards St. John, thus fronting the western sky. I saw no cross nor crucifix. On the body of the Lamb, and around it, I saw golden stars, or small brilliant lights, glittering like jets or glass balls, reflecting the light of some luminous body. I remained from a quarter past eight to half-past nine o'clock. At the time it was raining.

Fourth Witness.
Testimony of Patrick Walsh, aged Sixty-five years.

My name is Patrick Walsh; I live at Ballinderrig, an English mile from the chapel of Knock. I remember well the 21st of August, 1879. It was a very dark night. It was raining heavily. About nine o'clock on that night I was going on some business through my land, and standing a distance of about half a mile from the chapel, I saw a very bright light on the southern gabel-end of the chapel; it appeared to be a large globe of golden light; I never saw, I thought, so brilliant a light before; it appeared high up in the air above and around the chapel gable, and it was circular in its appearance; it was quite stationary, and it seemed to retain the same brilliancy all through. The following day I made inquiries in order to learn if there were any lights seen in the place that night; it was only then I heard of the Vision or Apparition that the people had seen,

Fifth Witness.

Testimony of Patrick Beirne, son of the elder Patrick Beirne, of Knock.

I am sixteen years of age; I live quite near the chapel; I remember well the evening of the 21st of August; it was Thursday, the evening before the Octave day. Dominick Beirne, Jun., a namesake of mine, came to my house, and said that he had seen the biggest sight that ever he witnessed in his life. It was then after eight o'clock. I came by the road on the west side of the church. I saw the figures clearly, fully, and distinctly—the Blessed Virgin, St. Joseph, and that of a bishop, said to be St. John the Evangelist. Young Beirne then told what he saw regarding the Vision, just as it has been described already by several persons who were present. The young fellow showed by his hands and position how the image or apparition of the Blessed Virgin Mary and that of St. Joseph and St. John stood.

I remained only ten minutes, and then I went away. All this happened between a quarter or so past eight o'clock and half-past nine.

Sixth Witness.

Testimony of Margaret Beirne, widow of Dominick Beirne, of Knock.

I, Margaret Beirne, *nee* Bourke, widow of Dominick Beirne, deceased, live near the chapel at Knock. I remember the evening of the 21st of August. I was called out at about a quarter past eight o'clock by my daughter Margaret to see the Vision of the Blessed Virgin Mary, and of the saints who appeared at the end of the little church; it was getting dark; it was raining. I came with others to the wall opposite the gable; I saw then and there distinctly the three images—one of the Blessed Virgin Mary, one of St. Joseph, and the third, as I learned, that of St. John the Evangelist. I saw an altar, too, and a Lamb on it, somewhat whiter than the altar; I did not see the cross on the altar. The Blessed Virgin Mary appeared in the attitude of prayer, with her eyes turned up towards heaven, a crown on her head, and an outer garment thrown round her shoulders. I saw her feet. St. Joseph appeared turned towards the Blessed Virgin, with head inclined· I remained looking on for fully fifteen or twenty minutes; then I left, and returned to my own house.

Seventh Witness.
The Testimony of Dominick Beirne.

I am brother of Mary Beirne, who has given her evidence already; I live near the chapel of Knock; my age is twenty years. On the occasion when my sister came at about eight o'clock on the evening of the 21st of August into our house, she exclaimed : " Come, Dominick, and see the image of the Blessed Virgin, as she has appeared to us down at the chapel." I said, " What image ?" and then she told me, as she has already described it for your reverence in her testimony : she told me all she was after seeing; I then went with her, and by this time some ten or twelve people had been collected around the place, namely, around the ditch or wall fronting the gable, where the vision was being seen, and to the south of the schoolhouse; then I beheld the three likenesses or figures that have been already described—the Blessed Virgin, St. Joseph, St. John, as my sister called the bishop, who was like one preaching, with his hands raised towards the shoulder, and the fore finger and middle finger pointedly set; the other two fingers compressed by the thumb; in his left he held a book; he was so turned that he looked half towards the altar and half towards the people; the eyes of the images could be seen: they were like figures, inasmuch as they did not speak. I was filled with wonder at the sight I saw; I was so affected that I shed tears; I continued looking on for fully an hour, and then I went away to visit Mrs. Campbell, who was in a dying state; when we returned the Vision had disappeared.

Eighth Witness.

Mrs. Hugh Flatley, widow of Hugh Flatley, states:—

I was passing by the chapel of Knock on the evening of the 21st of August, about eight o'clock, and I beheld most clearly and distinctly the figures of the Blessed Virgin Mary, St. Joseph, and that of St. John the Evangelist, standing erect at the gable-end of the chapel, towards the south side; I thought that the parish priest had been ornamenting the church, and got some beautiful likenesses removed outside.

Ninth Witness.

The Testimony of Bridget French, aged 75 (three score and fifteen) years.

The testimony of this witness was given in the Irish language. Her words were translated by Father Corbett into English while she spoke. The following is the version of what she said:—

My name is Bridget French; I live near the chapel of Knock. About half-past seven o'clock on the night of the 21st of August I was in the house of Mrs. Campbell, which is quite near to the chapel; while I was there Mary Beirne came in and said there was a sight to be seen at the chapel such as we never before beheld, and she told us all to come and see it; I asked her what it was, and she said that the Blessed Virgin, St. Joseph, and St. John were to be seen there. I went out immediately and came to the spot indicated. When I arrived there I saw distinctly the three figures. I threw myself on my knees and exclaimed: "A hundred thousand thanks to God and to the glorious Virgin that has given us this manifestation." I went in immediately to kiss, as I thought, the feet of the Blessed Virgin; but I felt nothing in the embrace but the wall, and I wondered why I could not feel with my hands the figures which I had so plainly and so distinctly seen. The three figures appeared motionless, statue-like; they were standing by the gable of the church in the background, and seemed raised about two feet above the ground. The Blessed Virgin was in the centre; she was clothed in white, and covered with what appeared one white garment; her hands were raised to the same position as that in which a priest holds his hands when praying at holy Mass. I remarked distinctly the lower portions of her feet, and kissed them three times; she had on her head something resembling a crown, and her eyes were turned up heavenwards. I was so taken with the Blessed Virgin, that I did not pay much attention to any other; yet I saw also the two other figures—St. Joseph standing to the right of the Blessed Virgin, or to the left, as I looked at him, his head bent towards her and his hands joined; and the other figure, which I took to be St. John the Evangelist, was standing at her left. I heard those around me say that the image was St. John. It was raining very heavily at the time, but no rain fell where the figures were. I felt the ground carefully with my hands, and it was perfectly dry. The wind was blowing from the south, right against the gable of the chapel, but no rain fell on that portion of the gable or chapel in which the figures were. There was no movement or active sign of life about the figures, and I could not say whether they were what living beings would in their place appear to be or not; but they appeared to me so full and so lifelike and so life-size that I could not understand why I could not feel them with my hands such as I beheld them with my eyes. There was an extraordinary brightness about the whole gable of the chapel, and it was observed by several who were passing along the road at the time. I remained there altogether about an hour, and when I came there first I thought I would never leave it. I would not have gone so soon as I did, but that I considered that the figures and that brightness would continue there always, and that on coming back I would again behold them. I continued to repeat the rosary on my beads while there, and I felt great delight and pleasure in looking at the Blessed Virgin. I could think of nothing else while there but giving thanks to God and repeating my prayers.

Tenth Witness.

Testimony of Catherine Murray, a girl of about eight years and six months, grand-daughter of Mrs. Beirne.

I am living at Knock; I was staying at my grandmother's. I followed my aunt and uncle to the chapel; I then saw the likeness of the Blessed Virgin Mary and that of St. Joseph and St. John, as I learned from those that were around about where I was; I saw them all for fully twenty minutes or thirty minutes.

Eleventh Witness.

Testimony of John Curry, a young boy, about six years old.

The child says he saw the images—beautiful images—the

Blessed Virgin and St. Joseph. He could state no more than that he saw the fine images and the light, and heard the people talk of them, and went upon the wall to see the nice things and the lights.

Twelfth Witness.

Testimony of Judith Campbell of Knock.

I live at Knock; I remember the evening and night of the 21st of August last. Mary Beirne called at my house about eight o'clock on that evening, and asked me to come to see the great sight at the chapel; I ran up with her to the place, and I saw outside the chapel, at the gable of the sacristy facing the south, three figures representing St. Joseph, St. John, and the Blessed Virgin Mary; also an altar, and the likeness of a Lamb on it, with a cross at the back of the Lamb. I saw a most beautiful crown on the brow or head of the Blessed Virgin. Our Lady was in the centre of the group, a small height above the other two; St. Joseph to her right, and bent towards the Virgin; St. John, as we were led to call the third figure, was to the left of the Virgin, and in his left hand he held a book; his right was raised with the first and second fingers closed, and the fore finger and middle finger extended as if he were teaching. The night came on, and it was very wet and dark; there was a beautiful light shining around the figures or likenesses that we saw. I went within a foot of them; none of us spoke to them; we believed they were St. Joseph and St. John the Evangelist, because some years ago statues of St. Joseph and of the Evangelist were in the chapel at Knock. All the figures were in white, or in a robe of silver-like whiteness; St. John wore a small mitre. Though it was raining, the place in which the figures appeared was quite dry.

Thirteenth Witness.

Testimony of Margaret Beirne.

I, Margaret Beirne, live near Knock chapel ; I am sister to Mary Beirne, who has seen the vision ; I remember the night of the 21st of August ; I left my own house at half-past seven o'clock, and went to the chapel and locked it ; I came out to return home ; I saw something luminous or bright at the south gable, but it never entered my head that it was necessary to see or inquire what it was; I passed by and went home. Shortly after, about eight o'clock, my niece, Catherine Murray, called me out to see the Blessed Virgin and the other saints that were standing at the south gable of the chapel. I went out then, and ran up to see what was to be seen. I there beheld the Blessed Virgin with a bright crown on her head, and St. Joseph to her right, his head inclined a little towards Our Blessed Lady, and St. John the Evangelist to her left, eastward, holding in his left hand a book of the Gospels, and his right hand raised the while, as if in the attitude of preaching to the people who stood before him at the ditch. The Virgin appeared with hands uplifted as if in prayer, with eyes turned towards heaven, and wearing a lustrous crown. I saw an altar there; it was surrounded with a bright light, nay, with a light at times sparkling, and so too were the other figures, which were similarly surrounded.

Fourteenth Witness.

Testimony of Dominick Beirne (senior).

I live at Knock; I remember the evening of the 21st of August; my cousin, Dominick Beirne, came to see us at about eight o'clock, P.M., and called me to see the vision of the Blessed Virgin Mary and other saints at the south gable of the chapel. I went with him. When I reached the south side of the chapel, we saw the image of the Blessed Virgin Mary, having her hands uplifted, and her eyes turned up towards heaven, as if in prayer, and she was dressed in a white cloak. To her right I saw St. Joseph, and on her left St. John, just as the other persons had told me before I came. I saw an altar there, and figures representing saints and angels traced or carved on the lower part of it. The night was dark and raining, and yet these images, in the dark night, appeared with bright lights as plain as under the noon-day sun. At the time it was pitch dark and raining heavily, and yet there was not one drop of rain near the images. There was a mitre on St. John's head, nearly like to that which a bishop wears. I was there only for one quarter of an hour; at the time I was there, five other persons were in it with me, looking on at the Apparition. All the figures appeared clothed in white; the whiskers on St. Joseph were an iron gray; the Blessed Virgin had on a white cloak. The reason I had for calling the third figure St. John is because some saw his statue or his likeness at Lekanvey parish chapel.

The fifteenth witness is John Durkan, one of the three who accompanied young Hill. His testimony is the same as that given by each of the Beirnes.

NOTE.—The Beirne family spell their name Beirn, or Beirne : correspondents spell the name "Byrne," which is in sound the same.

CHAPTER VI.

APPARITIONS IN OTHER COUNTRIES CONTRASTED WITH THAT AT KNOCK.

By many who do not believe in the supernatural, nay, by many who do not care to think that there is really another and a nobler life hereafter, these pages will be read.

Apparitions, such as those at Knock, those seen at Hartelwood, close to Marpingen, near the town of St. Wendel, in Bavaria, the apparitions so well known of La Salette, and of Lourdes, are strong reminders that there is a pure spirit world, a kingdom " to come," in which Jesus Christ reigns as King, and Mary his Mother, as Queen.

In all these supernatural manifestations there are features which mark them with a special character. Yet there are other features common to those revealed glimpses from spirit land, no matter whether they have been seen in times past or present, beheld in Ireland, or France, or Germany, or Italy, or Judea, or Egypt.

Characteristics of Supernatural Apparitions.

First, an apparition of an angel, or beatified soul, is always seen accompanied by light.

Secondly, the light appears first, and the supernatural being, or voice from amidst the light, next.

Thirdly, the heavenly messenger, or spirit disappears first, when the apparition ceases, and then immediately afterwards the light. These are a few of the objective features.

Instances compared with the Apparitions at Knock.

These three characteristics are found to mark the apparitions that have been seen at Knock, at Marpingen, at Lourdes, at La Salette; in every one of the spirit manifestations recorded in the "Lives of the Saints," and they are numerous, or in those we read of in the records of the Catholic Church, as, for instance, in the "Life of St. Columba, or Columbkille," the apostle of Scotland. He, like Abraham, walked continuously with angels, and talked with his spirit-guardians day after day. Whenever he was in his room alone, rays of light, although he had no lamp or source of material flame within, appeared to shine through the chinks of his cell.

The Burning Bush, seen by Moses, is an instance; and the Angel Gabriel, whom Daniel beheld in the land of captivity; the angelic choirs descending from heaven on the morning of the Nativity, and the bright light that shone around the shepherds; and the light on Thabor at the Transfiguration—these are proofs that the presence of angels and beatified souls is accompanied by light. Light, also, like the aurora before sunrise, is the herald of their coming, and as at sundown, the parting rays of day still illume the earth yet a little longer, so the departing messenger come from the world of beatified souls leaves for a time a bright line of radiance in his wake. This subject is very interesting, but just at present one can only touch the matter. It is singular, too, that it was on a Thursday that our Blessed Lady appeared at the Grotto of Massabielle, near Lourdes, to the young peasant girl, Bernadette Soubirous. February, 11th, 1858, was the day that the Virgin conceived without sin—"Immaculate Conception"—first appeared at Lourdes, and that day was Thursday. It is not much, but the coincidence is remarkable that it was on a Thursday she appeared at Knock—21st of August, 1879.

The Apparition in Bavaria.

The same day, July 3rd, 1876, that the image of the Immaculate Conception was crowned at Lourdes, at Marpingen, in Bavaria, the Blessed Virgin—"conceived without spot"—was pleased to manifest her presence to three young Catholic girls—Margaret Kunz, Susan Leist, and Catherine Hubertus.

Not to the Priest?

It is worthy of notice that not to the priest at Lourdes, or at Marpingen, or at La Salette, or at Knock has the Blessed Virgin been pleased to manifest her presence. People in this country have been expressing their surprise that, if the Apparition is true, "why did not the priest see it?" It has happened that Our Blessed Lady on each occasion has been pleased to appear to the simple people alone. On July 5th, 1876, the three young girls at Härtelwood asked the Blessed Virgin, who appeared to them that evening: "How long will you remain with us?" "Till ten o'clock." She remained at Knock on the 21st of August till ten o'clock. Again, they asked: "Shall our parish priest come?" "No." "Shall the priest of Hensweiler come?" "No." "Why are we alone able to see you?" "Because you are innocent children."

On July 11, the Blessed Virgin appeared again, and told the children that the sick were to take water from the upper well of the two wells in Härtelwood.

Some of the adult witnesses gave the following description of the Apparition with which they were favoured at Marpingen:—"The figure was that of a majestic woman, clothed in blue; it floated from the wood, and posed in an upright posture on the bush where the children had before seen her."

CHAPTER VII.

MANIFESTATIONS ON 6TH OF JANUARY AND 9TH OF FEBRUARY.

LIGHTS of a supernatural kind were beheld on the night of the 5th, or rather on the morning of the sixth, the feast of the Epiphany, January 6th, 1880. .They were seen by several, and especially by the police, who live convenient to the little church. Those guardians of peace went; out at 12 o'clock at night on patrol through the country to see that all was quiet, and came as far as Knock church, where they heard the hum of prayer arising from those who, at that midnight hour, had been assembled there in the hope of seeing the Apparition. The testimony of these sensible men, who took every precaution not to be deceived, who looked around the church and school, and hill and vale, mound and mearing, and saw no light, or reflection of light anywhere, but these extraordinary stars and globes of flame on the church gable before them, ought not readily to be discredited. The names of these servants of the Government are Collins and Fraher, one a native of Galway, the other of Tipperary.

Another remarkable Apparition appeared on the morning of the 10th of February. It was seen by several, especially by three young men from Claremorris, namely, John P. MacCloskey, Simon Conway, and Thomas MacGeoghegan, and by Martin Hession of Tuam, an intelligent assistant at Mrs. Murphy's establishment.

Young MacCloskey and the other two gave their spoken evidence in the presence of Joseph Bennett, Esq., special

correspondent of the *Daily Telegraph*, London. The annexed is the written testimony of John P. MacCloskey,
penned by himself, to which he signed his name. Young
MacCloskey has been remarkable from his childhood for his
guileless, honest, and pious course of life. He is now about
eighteen years. His testimony is confirmed by the separate
attestation of the other two, MacGeoghegan and Conway :—

I, John P. MacCloskey, a native of Claremorris, remember the night of the 9th of February, and the morning of the
10th. Simon Conway, MacGeoghegan, and I left Claremorris at 10 o'clock, P.M. We arrived at Knock sometime
after midnight ; our desire was to behold the Apparition.
After we had arrived, we continued to pray for some time.
At about three and a half o'clock on the morning of the 10th
of February, while I was praying before the gable of the Knock
chapel, I saw a light, like a white silvery cloud, move in a
slanting direction over from where the cross stands, on the
apex, and overspread the gable. In this bright cloud I saw
distinctly the figure and form of the Blessed Virgin Mary, so
clearly and fully that I perceived the fleshy colour of the feet.
Her dress resembled that made of white satin, and it contained numerous folds. The light had hardly settled on the
gable when it began to grow less bright, and to seem to fade
or darken in colour, leaving a wreath of its own brightness
still around the head of the Blessed Virgin, while the rest of
the gable became the colour of white paper stained with
pencil strokes. Every now and then a red tongue of flame
used to shoot down from the heavens and cross the gable.
During the momentary brightness resulting from these flashes,
the figure of the Blessed Virgin was each time fully seen.
In the absence of such flashes she was seen too, but not so
distinctly, only in subdued tones of colour. What attracted
my attention to the gable at first was small stars of an emerald

clear greenish colour, that appeared to go in and out through the gable, and at different parts of it. A star continued at intervals to twinkle right over the region of the Blessed Virgin's heart, and a little group of four or five stars were seen on the left side of the head. At no time did I see the countenance of Our Blessed Lady so clearly and distinctly as to be able to describe accurately the feature or the expression of the face. It was usually shrouded in light, and only at certain moments did I get a glimpse of full features.

The same evidence is given by Simon Conway, Thomas Geoghegan, Claremorris, and by several others.

Another witness, Mr. Martin Hession, Tuam.

I arrived about 6 o'clock, P.M., on Monday, the 9th of February, at Knock chapel. There was a large number of persons present. The evening was very wet and cold. I remained in the chapel for a considerable time. At 8 o'clock on that evening, at the south gable of the chapel I saw beautiful lights of many colours. They were at times exceedingly bright. Stars appeared both inside and outside the chapel. The lights continued coming and going until about half-past 6 o'clock next morning. At a quarter past 12 that night I saw a silvery cloud all over the gable of the chapel. After about five minutes it cleared off, and then immediately appeared three dark arches, and in the central one was the figure of a lady, which I took to be the Blessed Virgin. The figure was very beautiful. A mantle covered the figure all over: the mantle was white like satin, not a brilliant white. I saw two other figures, one on each side of the Blessed Virgin, but they were not quite distinct. A star of three different colours appeared under one of the figures: it was green, red, and white. The gable was, in fact, covered with stars. These appearances continued until about half-past 6 in the morning. I remained up all night looking at the figures and lights. I went in three times to the chapel to tell the people there to come out and see the lights. At about 5 o'clock in the morning three circles of stars appeared, as I thought, a half a mile over the top of the chapel. The circles of stars swayed to and fro in the air. There appeared at the same time over the cross on the gable of the chapel a row of stars which moved to the east of the gable and reached one of the figures which was said to be St. John. At about half-past 6 in the morning a shower of hail and rain came, and all who had been outside with myself went into the chapel, and at 7 o'clock, when I went out again, there was nothing to be seen of the beautiful lights.

I visited Knock again on the following Thursday, 12th February. It was dark when I reached there, and at about a quarter past 8 o'clock, went out from the chapel and looked at the gable. I was there but about ten minutes when I saw three figures of the shape of, but much larger than, those which I had seen on Monday night. The central figure was considered to be that of the Blessed Virgin. It was very brilliant. The other figures were not quite visible. After about five minutes they all disappeared. I went to the Archdeacon, met him on the road, and spoke to him about what I had just seen, and what I had seen on Monday night. Whilst speaking to him there appeared a beautiful star, which illuminated the whole place. The Archdeacon saw it, and he took off his hat, and asked me and a few others if we saw the light.

A Mayo Lourdes.

From the London "Daily Telegraph."

Some time ago a rumour began to prevail in Ireland that supernatural manifestations took place at or near the Catholic chapel of Knock, in the county Mayo. It was stated that an apparition of the Virgin Mary, attended by celestial personages, supposed to represent St. Joseph and St. John, had appeared to several persons on a certain night in August; subsequently to others on New Year's Eve, and a third time, to yet others, on the Eve of the Epiphany, and on the ninth of February. But this was not all. A further rumour stated that miracles of healing were frequently wrought upon sick persons who made pilgrimages and performed devotions at the favoured shrine, that miraculous virtues were possessed by the very plaster from the walls of the church, and that the faithful were crowding in ever-increasing numbers to the place thus suddenly dragged from obscurity into fame. So matters stood when, in the discharge of a mission connected with the Irish distress, I found myself at Claremorris, a little town about six miles from the much-talked-of village. It became my duty there to seek an interview with the parish priest—the Very Rev. Ulick J. Bourke, Canon of Tuam, and late President of St. Jarlath's College—a gentleman well known to philologists as the author of a learned work on the Aryan origin of the Gaelic race. Canon Bourke, having acted on a Commission appointed by the Archbishop of Tuam to take the evidence of those who asserted that they had seen the Apparitions, was well able to put me in the way of ascertaining particulars for myself, and within an hour of my introduction to him, I was face to face with one of the persons who deposed to the August vision.

One of the Witnesses.

This was a boy of about fourteen years of age, named Patrick Hill—a bright, intelligent little fellow, who told his tale clearly and simply. I shall put Hill's statement in the first person, without pledging myself, however, to literal exactness, and premising that the narrative was not continuous, but frequently interrupted by questions needless to repeat here : "I sometimes go out to the bog for turf, and did so on the day of the August Apparition, taking my little brother with me. When night came on, I went into the house of a relative, not far from Knock chapel. It was raining hard and very dark. While there someone (naming him), ran in and said: ' Oh, come up to the chapel, and see the Blessed Virgin against the wall !' We all ran up, and saw the end of the chapel covered with light; at first we stood against the wall of the yard, but presently we got over and went up close to the gable. Then we saw the Blessed Virgin standing like a statue so (lifting his hands and eyes); on her right was St. Joseph, bending towards her, and on her left St. John, dressed like a bishop, his left hand holding a book, his right raised, with two fingers pointing upwards. Above, and to the left of St. John, was an altar with a Lamb on it, round which moved what seemed to be the wings of angels, whose heads and bodies I could not see. We stood and looked at the figures a long time, and my little brother cried out that he wanted to take them home ; they did not move, but lights kept playing about the wall. Presently there were ten or eleven of us looking, and we all knelt down and said *Our Father*, and *Hail Mary* ; then, as the rain kept on, and we were very wet, we went away. I did not look behind me when standing in front of the figures, and cannot say whether any light was to be seen except on the wall." Having told this story in the manner already described, Hill departed, and presently a lad was brought in who witnessed the appearance in his company. The new-comer's statement did not agree in every detail with that of his predecessor, but substantially both were in accord; he, for example, saw no "angels' wings" fluttering round the Lamb, but only lights twinkling like stars. It was also stated that, though the rain beat against the chapel, the wall on which the light shone remained dry. To the question, "Did the figures look as though they were part of a picture ?" this witness replied, " No, they stood out from the wall like statues, and we seemed to see round them." To the further question, "Was the light on the gable a circle ?" he answered, " No ; it covered the wall."

Journeying to Knock.

On the morning after my interview with these early witnesses of the alleged marvel, I accepted Canon Bourke's invitation to drive over to Knock and see the place for myself. The five miles of road leading thither were not lonely. It was market-day in Claremorris, and the small farmers, who abound in that part of Mayo, were hastening townward with a multitude of asses bearing oats or potatoes or hay for sale at the advanced rates now " ruling." But all the travellers we met or passed were not on marketing thoughts intent. Some had an " up-all-night" appearance, and, indeed, had been keeping vigil in the chapel to which we were hastening ; while others, going the same way as ourselves, moved haltingly on foot, or swiftly on cars, in search of miraculous deliverance from the ills they suffered. The country thereabouts is uninteresting. It stretches west and east, in long undulations, without variety or charm. On reaching the summit of one of the gentle rises, a tall square tower appeared above the next eminence, and signalised our approach to Knock. The modest cottage of the parish priest, Archdeacon Cavanagh, lies in the intervening hollow; but before reaching it the traveller passes a thatched and whitewashed dwelling-house, bearing the distinguishing mark of a police-barrack. One of the stalwart members of the "Royal Irish" chanced to be standing in the road as we drove up, and him Canon Bourke introduced as a witness worth hearing.

The Policeman's Story.

The policeman cheerfully came round to my side of the car and told his story, in effect as follows :—"On a certain night (5th January, or morning of 6th—Epiphany), about twelve o'clock, I and a comrade set out on patrol, our road taking us past the chapel. When opposite the building we saw people, and heard the sound of praying, so we went in to look around and ascertain that all was right. Down to that time, though others professed to have witnessed the Apparitions, we had not. On going round to the east gable some one cried, 'There's the light,' and then both I and my comrade saw the end of the church covered with a rosy sort of brightness, through which what seemed to be stars appeared. I saw no figures, nor did my comrade; but some women, who were praying there, declared that they beheld the Blessed Virgin, and one went nearly frantic in consequence. We stood and watched the light for some time before starting again on our rounds." "How do you explain the light?" "I can't explain it." "Did you look around to see where it came from?" "I did; but everything was dark. There was no light anywhere, except on the gable." Thus the policeman, who offered to produce his comrade in corroboration.

The Parish Priest.

Leaving him, we drove to the cottage of the parish priest, and found him in his garden, whither he had gone, perhaps, for relaxation after getting through the multitude of letters that reach him by every post. Archdeacon Cavanagh is reputed along all the country side as a man of simple piety, gentle manners, and a modest and retiring disposition. This character is justified by his appearance; he at once makes a favourable impression, and is about the last man in the world whom a stranger would look upon and suspect of anything but straightforward, honest conduct. The very reverend gentleman gave his visitors a cordial welcome, and soon, in the little parlour of the cottage, I heard all that he could tell about the visions and miracles, in which he believes with unquestioning and reverent faith. As to the visions, the Archdeacon said, in effect: " On the night of the first Apparition my housekeeper asked leave to visit a friend, and remained out unusually late. While wondering what had become of her, she made her appearance in a very excited state, exclaiming: 'Oh! your reverence, the wonderful and beautiful sight! The Blessed Virgin has appeared up at the chapel, with St. Joseph and St. John, and we have stood looking at them this long time. Oh! the wonderful sight!' Inferring that the vision had disappeared, and omitting to question my housekeeper on that point, I did not go up, and I have regretted ever since that I omitted to do so. On another occasion a messenger was sent down to fetch me: I was in bed after a fatiguing day, and, having a prospect of hard work on the morrow, did not rise."—This manifestly appears as a triumph of the flesh over the spirit.—" I shall ever feel sorry that a sight of the Apparitions has been denied me, but God may will that the testimony to his Blessed Mother's presence should come from the simple faithful and not through the priests. Though I have not witnessed the divine manifestation I have seen the light, and once, when standing at some distance from the chapel, in company with others, a most brilliant star flashed along the gable, leaving a train of radiance."

Miraculous Cures.

Questioned as to miracles, the archdeacon said : " I will show you a long list of cures effected by the divine interposition, and can tell you of one in which I was an agent. Some little while ago I received a ' sick-call ' late at night to a man who was said to be vomiting blood, and in extreme danger. Hastening to the house, attended by a boy with a lantern, I met the father of the patient coming to hurry me, in distress lest I should be too late. On reaching the cottage, I found the young man covered, so to speak, with blood, and apparently very near death, but conscious. After ministering to him, I called for a glass of water, sprinkled on it a few particles of the mortar from the gable wall of the chapel, and bade him drink. He did so ; at once he began to recover, and is now well. I can speak of other cases, but especially of a man who came from Cork afflicted with a polypus, which extended into his windpipe, and so, said the surgeons, required a dangerous operation. He was here performing his devotions for several days, and then, to his astonishment and joy, expelled the abnormal growth—I saw it—and he returned cured." The archdeacon next showed me his list of "miracles," from which I quote a few special cases: Bridget Nearney of Strokestown, blind for seventeen years, can see ; Maria Conolly, a cripple for thirteen years, is now able to walk ; John O'Brien, who was born blind, has the use of his eyes; Belinda Mash of Ballina, dumb for six years, has recovered the power of speech; Patrick Boyle, of Glasgow, came to Knock afflicted with heart disease, and returned cured; Michael Marin of Lisakullen, subject to epileptic fits, visited the shrine, and is now free from their attacks; the daughter of R. Walsh of Clifden, regained sight after bathing her eyes in water containing a piece of plaster from the chapel wall; John Roache of Roosky, Roscommon, stone blind for seventeen years, went away able to see; John O'Connor of Ardagh, came to Knock with a bent leg, supported by an iron crutch, and returned home, leaving the crutch as a memorial of cure; Owen Halpen, of Meg, Drogheda, troubled with deafness, placed a bit of the mortar in his ears, and had the sense fully restored to him. I might continue these extracts from the archdeacon's records, but space would fail for a complete setting forth of the alleged cases of miraculous hearing.

Magic Lantern light not possible in the situation.

Leaving the priest's cottage to view the chapel, and meeting at the door a man whose sight, long lost, was said to be returning, the two priests and myself went up the road towards the chapel, having the famous gable before us the whole way. I saw that, for full half its height, it had been boarded over—a measure necessary, the archdeacon told me, to protect the wall, since the people, after having removed the covering of plaster, began to pick the mortar from between the stones, as, indeed, they are now doing round the corners, where nothing prevents. My first business was, of course, to take, as Jack Bunsby would say, "the bearings" of the place. The chapel is a plain cruciform building, having a tall, square tower at its west end, and at the opposite extremity a sacristy. It is on the gable of the sacristy, at the far east of the building, that the figures are said to have appeared.

The chapel stands in a rather extensive yard, which is bounded, opposite the gable, and distant from it some twenty-five paces, by a dilapidated wall about four feet high. Beyond this is a large field and the open country. Within the yard, a little to the north of a line drawn from the north angle of the gable to the low wall, stands a schoolhouse, its gable directly facing towards the east. Obviously, therefore, if the appearances alleged to have been seen on the chapel wall were due to a magic lantern, the operator, supposing he could have focussed his picture at such a distance, must have taken post behind the low wall; or, if stationed in the school, must have thrown the image on the " screen " at a very considerable angle. The wall theory may be dismissed, because over its tumbled stones the first witnesses passed to get a nearer view, and the glare of the lantern would at once have been detected by the observant policemen. There remains the notion of a manipulator stationed in the schoolhouse. I gave my best attention to the windowless gable of that building, and could find no sign of hole or crack from chimney to foundation. Going inside among the children, to look at the wall from that point of view, the plaster appeared untouched, and the roof too much open to admit of a man working between its apex and what there was of ceiling. In the result, and despite a wish to explain the wonder naturally, I was obliged to conclude that the reported Apparitions, however caused, could not have been, and, therefore, were not, due to a magic lantern. With any theory not determinable by a reference to considerations absolutely positive, such as those just touched upon, I have nothing now to do.

Scenes at the Church.

Mondays and Thursdays are the times when Knock is overwhelmed with pilgrims, many thousands being frequently present at once; but on no day of the week is the place deserted, and it assuredly afforded an extraordinary spectacle last Wednesday. About ten paces from the gable stands a small roughly-constructed pen, wherein pilgrims who no longer require the aid of sticks and crutches deposit them before leaving. Scores of these discarded props to tottering feet were lying there; and a few others, besides two very battered umbrellas, were suspended from the boards that protect the sacred wall. It is needless to say that the wall itself, boarded though it be, excites the utmost reverence. I saw a score of people kneeling before it repeating prayers, some of them knowing the spot on which they believe the Virgin appeared; while others had brought sick children, upon whom they lavished attention in the intervals of devotion. Others, again, wandered round and round the chapel, telling their beads as they went—an act of faith, so I was assured, altogether self-imposed. Yet others, mostly afflicted with diseases, stood about in the road, or enclosure, waiting, like some at the Pool of Bethesda long ago, " for the moving of the waters." Night and day they wait, filling the chapel during the dark hours, and praying there so as that the sound of their voices can be heard far down the road. At least two hundred persons were in the sacred edifice when I entered. The interior is poor of aspect. Beyond the unpretending altar, and two or three small windows filled with stained glass, there are no attempts at decorations, and very ineffective ones at convenience, since all the benches in the place would not seat more than thirty people. The floor is roughly flagged and full of holes made by devotees who, in their eagerness to possess some blessed substance, have dug beneath the level of the stones. But, holes or no holes, the pilgrims covered almost the entire area, from the altar rails to the western door and from side to side of the transept, their muttered petitions making a continuous and solemn hum. Many sick have been brought there, and some professed to have gained much benefit. A poor paralytic, seated in a wheeled chair, rejoiced at a feeling of warmth in his lower limbs; a woman, who had crawled for years on her hands and knees, was found sitting upright, and delightedly showing how she could use her feet a very little. Such sights were visible more or less on every hand, and as the archdeacon went about among the people one and another would go to him and tell of the benefits received by themselves or their friends, and get for answer : " Thank God and his Blessed Mother."

My story is told, and I have nothing more to say. The conclusion to be drawn from it one way or another is the business of the reader.

CHAPTER VIII.

MIRACLES.

IN a *brochure* the size of the present issue no explanation of miracles can be expected; yet, it is well to state for the general reader that the definition of miracles, as understood by Catholics, requires that it be an extraordinary work or operation opposed to the normal laws of nature, and performed either directly or indirectly by God. The work must be unusual, for, if usual, although the effect of great power, it is not considered a miracle. The movements of the planets and of the earth, with their amazing velocities, are not miracles, although they are a prodigious work. But to carry a man in the air from this to New York in a minute would be a miracle. The work must be opposed to the laws of nature, either contrary to them or above their influence. It is natural for fire to burn; for a body heavier than water to sink in it. If a body be not burned in the fire, like the three companions of Daniel in the fiery furnace; and our blessed Lord walking on the waters of the sea of Genesareth—that is a miracle; and it must be done by God's power either directly, as the miracles performed by Christ; or indirectly, as those performed by Moses and the prophets in the name of God, and by the apostles and their successors in the name of Jesus. This definition excludes all works done by the agency of the devil or his agents, all necromancers, sorcerers, enchanters, who invoke his name. It is not necessary here to tell what the laws of nature are; it is quite enough to know that it is a law in fire to burn; in water to quench fire and to wet the surface on which it is placed unless some other natural cause is in the way to prevent the effect; in a heavy, sluggish body not to move quickly; in a sickly body not to assume strength suddenly, and by means not proportionate to the effect. Any effect contrary to these, or superseding these laws, is said, as far as relates to man, to be supernatural. An effect of this kind would not for a spirit be supernatural, because it is just suited to his nature; but, in regard to man, effects like these are supernatural. From all that has been said, it is plain that a cure brought about by a strong imagination is not a miracle, for it is only a natural effect; neither is a cure arising from a sudden start or excitement, as, for instance, if a dumb person from fright, or from a sudden impulse, spoke—that is not a miracle, because it is the natural result of great physical excitement. If, too, owing to some cause, either the hearing, or the eyesight, or the voice, was partially lost by any nervous derangement, as often happens, if that derangement be set right, and that the hearing is restored, the eye has obtained its usual power of seeing, and the tongue its speech from a strengthened glottis, that is not a miracle. If the effect has been produced by a natural cause, adequate in the circumstances to achieve the result, or if it is a work from the demon, it cannot be pronounced a miracle. But, if it is from God or his agents, and done in the name of God, and for a good purpose, even by a natural cause, but a natural cause inadequate of itself to the end, then it is a miracle, as, for instance, the case of the blind man who was desired by the Redeemer to go to the pool of Siloe and to wash; and he went, he washed, and he saw; or the miraculous effects of St. Peter's shadow, or St. Paul's handkerchief.

Of course many people do not believe in spirit or angel, or in God's power, or in the power abiding in his Church;

to them miracles are shams, or they are put by them in the category of spirit-rapping and of jugglery. But Christians know that there is a spirit-world, happy souls and angels, that there is a God who guides and directs everything, who seeks the love and devotion, as well as the happiness of his intelligent creatures—all mankind. We are the principal object of the care and loving attention of God, and for our sakes, and to excite our faith and love, He performs miracles. His children regard them—miracles—as the seal and language of God speaking to the heart of man. Is there a miracle there? Then, if so, it is God's voice, at least to those who believe in Him: it is a light from heaven, and the pure-eyed soul sees that light and believes it as the expression of God to him. But all do not believe in miracles with equal readiness. Christ performed them, and the Pharisees attributed their performance to the power of the prince of devils. Moses performed them, and Pharaoh resisted him the more determinedly. It is so to-day. It does not follow that if some people believe not in miracles that they have not really been performed.

The question now is, Has any real miracle been performed at Knock?

We answer that in our opinion there have been many. A great many cures will, or perhaps can be traced to nervous excitement, and to the desire for improvement; but making all due allowances for physical agencies and natural causes, still over one-third of those recorded will, it is likely, be considered, in the opinion of honest men, miraculous.

The diary which is kept by Archdeacon Cavanagh contains a record of nigh three hundred; ten select miracles out of this number would plainly prove the miraculous character of the Apparitions witnessed on the several occasions recorded in the pages of the Very Rev. Archdeacon Cavanagh's diary.

Cases of Cure, from Archdeacon Cavanagh's Diary.

On Thursday, 11th March, the writer saw at Knock a young man named Anthony Cavanagh, from 15 Brabazon-street, Dublin, who declared, in the presence of clergymen and gentlemen of the highest position and literary standing, that for eleven years he could not stir one foot without the aid of crutches, walk as well as anyone can walk, except that the right leg was still short, although it had regained its natural strength.

On the same day the writer, and the witnesses with him, saw at Knock chapel a woman, aged about twenty-eight, who had been deaf since she was six years old, receive the power of hearing. The writer spoke to her, and she heard as well as anyone gifted with the faculty of hearing.

Miss Glynn, Kilkerrin, housekeeper to Rev. John M'Greal, C.C., Lavallyroe, Ballyhaunis; pains and general debility.

Frank Conway, Eden; arm powerless.

Peter Murphy, Newtown, near Claremorris; cured of lameness.

Mrs. Fitzgerald, Swinford; general debility.

Pat Boyle, of Garlagh, parish of Crossboyne; epilepsy.

Mary Devine, Ballyhaunis, a girl of eleven; lameness and an evil.

Miss Mannion, of the parish of Roscommon; sight improved by a visit to the church.

Michael Langan, a man in the employment of Mr. Little; chronic pain in the foot.

Michael MacHale, of Killala; nearly blind; power of seeing much better.

John Fogarty of Crusheen; weakness of the left foot.

Pat Ryder of Craughwell; epilepsy.

Michael Brennan, Ballyhaunis ; palsy of the head.

Michael Ansbro, Carramore ; restored to sight.

Mrs. Kelly, Claremorris ; cured of a constant pain in the side.

Kate Rodgers ; consumption ; used to faint every day for a considerable time ; is quite restored to health.

Mrs. Feeny, hotel-keeper, Swinford ; violent toothache ; cured by an application of the cement.

Mrs. (Martin) Fleming of Tubber, Ballina ; sore leg.

Mary Gallagher, Charleston, county Mayo, blindness. After visiting Knock she was restored to sight.

A young man from Charleston, county Mayo, cured of an evil by a visit to Knock, after doctors had entirely failed to help him.

Laurence Fleming, parish of Dunmore ; cured of deafness.

John Kelly of Ballina ; chronic pain in the right side.

A young man named Hopkins, second assistant in the National School, Claremorris ; cured of epilepsy.

John Smith, parish of Virginia (Rev. John O'Reilly, P.P.), county Cavan ; general weakness of constitution, loss of appetite, and want of sleep.

John Coan, Plougena, county Mayo ; paralysis.

Thomas Hare, Tuam ; paralysis.

Pat Ryan, Edward-street, Limerick ; defective sight.

Francis Cassidy, Maguire's Bridge ; paralysis of the left hand.

Lizzie Bryan, Drumtraff, county Cork ; evil and swelling in the jaw.

Mrs. Healy, Drumtraff; an evil.

Thomas Crogan ; sore foot.

Mary Vesey, Betley, England ; lameness. She left her crutch at Knock.

James O'Connell, parish of Drumlish ; blindness.

John Meckin ; blindness. He was not entirely blind

before his visit to Knock, but his power of vision was very feeble.

William Conway, King's County; pain in the heart and stomach, from which he had been suffering for years.

Daniel Ren, Queen's County; sore in the leg; had suffered from it for fourteen years.

John Shanahan, parish of Adare, county Limerick; swelling in the right knee.

Marie Shields, Loughrea; defective sight.

John Farrell, Castlerea; constant pain and stiffness in the knee.

Sarah Morrisroe of Woods, parish of Ballaghy; paralysis. Mr. Ignatius O'Donel of Swinford bears testimony to her case in the following terms : "I saw her myself on or about the 22nd December, when she had not the use of her limbs, and on seeing her yesterday, after she had walked seven miles, she did not seem to be a bit tired.—Ignatius O'Donel, Swinford, February 5th, 1880."

Jeremiah Sullivan, parish of Rathbarry, Clonakilty, county Cork ; polypus, or flesh growth in the windpipe. He came to Knock with his father on Sunday, the 1st of February, and got rid of his disease on the 4th. The following is his statement to Archdeacon Cavanagh :—"I have been suffering from a hoarseness for the last eighteen months. I consulted four of the neighbouring doctors, one after the other, and to no avail, as none of them were able to ascertain the nature of the disease. Finding myself daily getting worse I came to the city of Cork, and consulted the most eminent doctor there. On the third day he found my ailment proceeded from a flesh growth or polypus in the windpipe. The conclusion the doctor came to was that there should be an operation, either externally or internally, either of which would be very dangerous. Hearing of the apparition of the Blessed Virgin Mary at Knock, I decided on visiting the place. I arrived on Sunday morning, February 1st. Thanks be to God and to the Blessed Virgin Mary, I coughed off the polypus on the morning of the 4th February, after my third day's visit here."

Pat Scott of Ballymoe, has made the following declaration :—"I, Pat Scott, parish of Ballintubber, county Roscommon, do hereby solemnly declare that it is at Knock I received power in my leg, which was not of the least use to me for upwards of eight and a-half years, being entirely powerless. I could not move or walk without a crutch. I can now walk firmly on it, but it is still short. Ballintubber, 31st January, 1880." The following is an extract from a letter lately written by Pat Scott to the Ven. Archdeacon Cavanagh:—

"DEAR FATHER CAVANAGH,—

"It is with great pleasure I write an answer to yours, which I received a few days ago, but must make an apology for delaying so long referring to the particulars you require to know from me. The facts are simply these : Nine years ago I was attacked with a pain in my groin, and for five months no one could tell whether I would live or die. The summer after I was enabled to move very slowly by means of a crutch, which I continually carried for the last successive eight years, to the day in question. During that time my leg, down from my hip, was quite powerless, but had feeling. I could not go to my bedside without the aid of the crutch. I never walked on the heel, but simply tipping the ground with the top of my toe, in consequence of a contraction of the sinews. Mrs. —— induced my mother to send me to Knock, that holy place, and on entering the chapel the second time on the same day I discovered the leg gaining strength. I was so much rejoiced that I determined to leave the crutch after me, as I did, and for the first time out of nine years made the effort of walking, independent of the crutch, with both heel and toe, to the astonishment of all the neighbours here, who looked upon me as a very great miracle and curiosity. I forgot to say I carried a stick, and still do. I find I am every day improving, but I do not feel so well satisfied till I pay one or two visits more to Knock. There is no doubt but I derived this great blessing from our Immaculate and Heavenly Queen.

"I am, reverend sir,

"Very respectfully yours,

"PAT SCOTT."

www.ingramcontent.com/pod-product-compliance
Lightning Source LLC
Chambersburg PA
CBHW030007030726
47499CB00008B/2934